Praise for
Kristine Kathryn Rusch

"A dark, yet fascinating tale, *The Enemy Within* gives readers an intriguing look at what could have happened in 1964 New York."
—*RT Book Reviews* on *The Enemy Within*

"Deeply evocative, it breathes menace from every page and memorably conveys what Rusch calls the 'casual evil' that suffused Germany as the Nazis came to power."
—The *Daily Mail* (London)
on *Hitler's Angel*

"Told in roughly alternating chapters set in 1913 and 2005, *[Snipers]* is a deft mixture of SF and mystery with some very sharp plotting, some nice twists, and a trio of compelling characters."
—*Booklist,* starred review, on *Snipers*

"Rusch is best known for her Retrieval Artist series, but occasionally she gives us a standalone gem like *Snipers*…. *Snipers* is a riveting suspense tale and a fine SF story—what more could we want?"
—*Analog* on *Snipers*

Also by

Kristine Kathryn Rusch

THE FAERIE JUSTICE SERIES

Show Trial (novella)
The War and After (short-story collection)

OTHER HISTORICAL FICTION

Hitler's Angel
Snipers
The Enemy Within
The Tower (novella)

SHOW TRIAL

A FAERIE JUSTICE NOVELLA

KRISTINE KATHRYN RUSCH

*wmg*PUBLISHING

Show Trial

Published 2015 by WMG Publishing
www.wmgpublishing.com
First published in *Subterranean Online*, Spring, 2011
Cover art copyright © Philcold/Dreamstime
Book and cover design copyright © 2015 by WMG Publishing
Cover design by Allyson Longueira/WMG Publishing
ISBN-13: 978-0-615-81925-9
ISBN-10: 0-615-81925-7

SHOW TRIAL

A FAERIE JUSTICE NOVELLA

1

LATER HE POURED OVER OLD NEWSPAPERS, *LIFE* AND *TIME* magazines, and the newsreel footage kept by the War Department, looking for her, even though someone told him she couldn't be photographed. Still, he thought he saw her in at least two of the attempted Hitler assassination sites—as part of the 1939 crowd in the Munich Burgerbraukeller, and bringing coffee to the men at the 1944 Wolf's Lair meeting. Sometimes he saw a swirl of light, and thought he caught a glimpse of her inside it—just a bit of black hair, a touch of skirt.

He told them to watch out for her in Nuremberg for the remaining trials, but of course, she never appeared there again.

She should never have appeared there at all.

2

HE FIRST MET HER IN PARIS, AUGUST, 1945. HE HAD NO WAY to describe how he felt then. "World-weary" was too weak a term, "depressed" too passive, and "defeated" put him on the wrong side. From the outside, he looked the same as he always had: Lieutenant Robert Parker in full dress uniform, square shoulders, square jawed, handsome in an All-American sort of way.

When he enlisted, his mother had brushed off those shoulders, tears in her eyes, saying, *You look so grown-up*, forgetting that he had already grown-up—a full-fledged college professor with a newly minted PhD. Twenty-seven years old, unmarried to his mother's chagrin, oldest of seven children—five of them boys. He looked so grown-up then, and he had felt so grown-up, but he hadn't known grown-up.

Some people never knew grown-up. They went through life doing what they were supposed to, getting married, raising children, contributing to their communities. They never shot at anyone at close range, had a friend bleed out beneath their helpless hands, or march into hell to save hundreds of skeletons standing next to piles of stinking corpses.

Some people never understood the dark side of life, and he wasn't going to teach them. But he wasn't sure how he would return to the lighter side or if he even could. Laughing surprised him and, oddly, Paris offended him.

It was so perfect—still the city he had seen in college. Sure, some windows were shattered, stoops broken, signs missing or torn down. The population was thinner, the clothing styles similar to the ones he'd seen nearly a decade before. But the city itself had no rubble, no stray dogs digging up rotted limbs from bomb craters, no children playing in the remains of houses. Even the food seemed good compared with the rest of Europe, although he really wasn't one to judge. He'd been in Germany since January, and Germany was one gigantic bomb crater.

As it should be.

He didn't want Paris to be destroyed. He had loved the city, back when he had been the kind of man who could love something. But he felt that Paris should have paid a price for her collaboration, for all the people it had sent to the camps, people whom he had seen either standing listlessly near a gate or stacked like cordwood outside so-called barracks.

He would never shake those days from his mind, never, and he couldn't talk about them either. Sometimes he imagined sitting at his mother's pristine dining room table as she placed the Thanksgiving turkey in the middle like something out of the *Saturday Evening Post*, his siblings and their spouses clutching the good silver around the even better china, waiting for the feast.

What did you do during the war, Robert? someone would ask politely, and he would say, he would say—

I learned that sometimes you saw so much it leached the empathy from you, so much that all you could do was turn away, and wonder what kind of monster would do this. And then I realized I had met the monsters that ordered this, talked with them, laughed with a few of them, and they hadn't seemed like monsters at all. You'd think their eyes would be different, their lips would curl upwards revealing fangs. You'd think they would smell of death, but they were often perfumed, rich, charming. It was their victims that smelled of death.

Surprisingly, to him, Paris made these thoughts worse. As he walked down the Champs-Elysée, he would see—in his mind's eye—the Nazis marching through, just as he had seen in the newsreels, the Nazi flag hanging from the Arc de Triomphe, the German soldiers leaning against the Eiffel Tower as if they had built it themselves.

And now that he was here, in a city where the Germans had been vanquished almost a year ago, a city that was quiet and lovely and seemed so very civilized, he felt angrier than he ever had. It was as if the city had taken his numbness and turned it inside out, revealing it for the cocoon it had been.

He wasn't guarded any more.

He didn't need to be. He had been on the winning side, after all.

The winning side.

As if anyone had won.

He hadn't expected Paris to be hot in August, but it was. Before the war, he had come to Paris in the fall because his professors had warned him to stay away in the summer—not because of the heat, but because the French took the month of August off. He wondered if they had done that during the war. The famously rigid Germans probably had not allowed it.

So this August, the city's emptiness should have been profound. But it was not. On his first free day, he took his lunch in the Tuileries garden and watched children play. Mothers, nannies, he couldn't tell which, supervising and laughing as if they didn't have a care in the world.

Old men lounged on benches near the Louvre, and somewhere in the back, the screech of a Punch and Judy show went on as if it had never been silenced. He had bought himself a ham sandwich which in Paris wasn't two thin slices of white bread over processed meat, but a baguette with rich butter, a thick slab of cheese, and cured meat that had more flavor than anything he'd ever had back home—anything he'd had, truly, since the war began.

Still, he couldn't eat. He looked at the beautiful garden, which had been one of Paris's treasures since Louis XIV's gardener laid it out in the early 1700s, and thought how the beautiful historic gardens of London had burned or still had unexploded bombs in the middle of them. He didn't see the beauty of the Tuileries—he couldn't see the beauty—because he knew it had been built on a betrayal so profound that he wasn't sure he would ever be able to forgive this city he had once loved. Even though she still looked like herself. Even though everything he loved about her remained—except, perhaps, her soul.

At that moment, he saw her coming out of the Metro, and for a moment, he thought she was a human manifestation of the city itself. Tall, thin and oh-so-French. Her tan skirt was a bit frayed, but it still flared around stunning legs. Her shoes were scuffed, but the heels showed off her ankles. Her blouse was a starched pale pink which accented her slightly dusky skin. Her shoulder-length black hair swayed as she walked.

She was no different than the other women leaving the Metro, heading toward the Louvre on their lunch break, and yet she was. Because behind those fine cheekbones, behind the half-smile on her lips, was a light that he had never seen before. It was as if she had swallowed a bit of the sun, and its rays emanated through her pores.

He had never seen anyone so beautiful, so ethereal, and yet so practical and solid. Like the city herself, stunning and down-to-earth all at the same time.

He was on his feet before he realized it—standing, about to cross the garden—when he couldn't see her any longer. She had been there, and then she was gone as if she had never been.

He turned toward the old men, dozing in the hot noon-time sun, but clearly none of them had seen her. He looked up and down the rue di Rivoli, but he didn't see her.

He knew that people vanished like that all the time. You took your eye off them for a single moment, and they turned a corner or ducked into a shop, and you never saw them again.

But he hadn't taken his eyes off her. He had been watching her, studying her if truth be told, trying to memorize her, and she had winked away as if someone had turned out her inner light.

The incident left him a little shaken; he was more tired than he thought possible. He sat back down, opened the butcher paper surrounding his sandwich and ate it slowly, savoring every bite.

He had promised himself, after the horror of the camps, that he would enjoy each moment of his life, but he had broken that promise as the Army Jeep drove him away. He hadn't enjoyed a single moment—he wasn't sure if he still could.

But he would try.

He was in Paris. It was beautiful, and he would try.

3

HIS COMMANDING OFFICER HAD ORDERED PARKER TO take two days of rest once he got to Paris, but Parker didn't want to rest. He couldn't really, not when there was so much to do.

They had ten weeks to find translators good enough, smart enough, flexible enough to take on a brand new challenge. Plus these translators had to be willing to move to Germany for the duration of a trial, and they had to have strong stomachs, because they would learn what Parker had learned.

First he talked with former colleagues at the Sorbonne, those who remained, those who had been too old, too frightened, too useless to help with translations during the war. They had several prospective candidates for him, most of whom specialized in literature in translation.

He needed translators who could work with documents because every piece of paper the court turned out needed to be in the official languages of the Tribunal: French, German, English, and Russian. Just before he had left for Paris, he had heard that the judges were arguing about the manner in which the trial would be conducted.

If four powers agreed to run the trial using the Continental system, then the translators wouldn't deal with witnesses. Everything—from testimony to documents— would be handed to the magistrates as a dossier. The dossier would determine the charges (if any) and the manner of the trial which, so far as he knew, would then consist of more dossiers and very little testimony in front of the court. He wasn't completely certain how all of this would work—that was for the judges to decide—but they had explained things well enough for him to understand that from a translation point of view, this system was the best.

But the Americans and the British wanted to use their legal tradition instead of the French and Russian system. Parker was familiar with that. Very familiar, since he had done some translation work in court while working on his Ph.D. The Anglo-American system would be much more interesting for journalists and the public. And, no matter what the officials claimed, this trial was designed to show the world that the rule of law had returned. The age of dictators and mass murder was over.

He wanted it to be true. He really did. And that was why he hadn't gone home when he had the chance. He had reupped to help with the cleanup.

Besides, he wasn't in any shape to return to the Land of the Free and the Home of the Brave.

So, instead, he focused on language, and more importantly, the use of language. Supreme Court Justice Robert Jackson, who was in charge of this whole thing for the Americans, wanted the trial to be translated for *everyone* in real time. Parker had thought that impossible until a few weeks ago. Then Colonel Leon Dostert mentioned a simultaneous translation system he'd worked with at the first meeting of the United Nations in April, using some kind of technology where everyone would have headphones and everyone could hear a translation of speech and testimony in their own language while someone was speaking.

Parker hadn't believed that he could listen and translate at the same time, but Dostert had tested him repeatedly, and Parker could. He was young enough, Dostert said, and had a nimble mind. But it was more than that. Parker could almost feel his brain splitting into two parts—one part listening and one part searching for the right word. He actually liked doing the work. It was one of the few things that had challenged him since the war ended.

But, he soon learned, most people with a facility for language couldn't simultaneously translate. Not even people trained in consecutive translation. Particularly people trained in consecutive translation. They had been taught to listen first, take notes, and then translate the notes, carefully and quickly, choosing the very best words.

In simultaneous, there was no time for the best words. Only the words that came first. And that, more than anything, was what the legal minds were worried about. Incorrect translation.

If the judges running this tribunal decided on the Anglo-American method—and ended up using simultaneous translation—then Dostert estimated that the tribunal would need a minimum of 200 translators, working in all areas from documents to consecutive translation to simultaneous translation.

Parker couldn't imagine managing 200 translators, particularly since the tribunal wouldn't just need English, German, French, and Russian translators. They would need translators who spoke Dutch and Hungarian, Spanish and Portuguese, all of the languages of Europe and maybe even more. He was supposed to find a range and depth of people that he wasn't even sure existed, and then he was supposed to ask them to work in a system that hadn't really been invented yet.

The professors at the Sorbonne said this would be impossible, and Parker was inclined to agree. Still, he had his orders and he had his mission. The professors would give him a list of student names by the following day, and any professor who was interested would also sign up for tests.

Then, one of them had a suggestion that changed everything.

He recommended that Parker go to the Paris International Telephone Exchange. There, he said, no one cared about linguistic accuracy. They cared about putting the call through.

Parker knew he had just suffered a very French put-down: *if he didn't care about accuracy (and of course, an*

American wouldn't), then leave the Sorbonne. Go somewhere that doesn't have time to care, somewhere somewhat American. Go to somewhere plebian. Go to the phone exchange.

And so he did.

4

IT TOOK HIM A WHILE TO FIND IT. THE PARIS INTERNATIONAL Telephone Exchange did not advertise its existence, probably a byproduct of the war. If no one knew where the exchange was, then no one could bomb it or attack it or do anything to disrupt it.

He had to go to through U.S Army Headquarters to get the information, as if the location of the Phone Exchange was still a closely guarded secret.

The building itself had no signage. It looked like many other Parisian buildings built in the early part of the century—the cool white brick of the Belle Epoch era without any of the frills. Still, it blended into its neighborhood, looking cool and majestic behind a tree-lined sidewalk, off a wide street.

The calm quiet of the exterior didn't prepare him for the interior. He stepped into heat and chaos covered with a metallic stench he recognized from military outposts. Someone was running a lot of equipment here, and the equipment it-self gave off a smell of overheated metal, a smell that made him so nervous he almost turned around and left.

The reception area was small and narrow; it had clear-ly once been an entrance hallway. Photographs hung on the walls, mostly photographs of telephones, although some were of people talking on telephones. Most were ad-vertisements of some kind, clipped and put into frames. The hallway had a flat runner that had once been red, but clearly hadn't been cleaned in months (maybe years).

As he got closer to the desk, the smell of cigarettes and coffee greeted him. A young thin man sat at the desk, his brown eyes large and shadowed.

His gaze ran up and down Parker's green uniform, and his expression grew disdainful.

"What?" he asked in English.

Not *what do you want?* or even *Hello*, but *What*? Parker felt a moment of exasperation, even though he was used to the attitude. The young man expected Parker to be a gum-chewing, glad-handing GI, destructive and strong and not very bright.

"*Bonjour*," he said in his most perfect Parisian French, and then proceeded to ask—in as snotty a tone as he could manage—for the person in charge.

"I am sure I can help you, sir," the young man re-sponded in English, deciding to take on (and win) the linguistic battle.

Parker continued to speak French. He said that he was certain that a receptionist did not have the ability to deal with an important request from General Eisenhower himself. Parker almost said from the President himself, but figured that General Eisenhower—one of the liberators of France—would have a lot more pull here.

The young man glared at him, then nodded once. "You are correct, sir. For a request that important, you must speak with Monsieur LeRoi."

Then the young man left his post, but not before grabbing his half-smoked Camel, testifying to both his poverty and his own difficulties during the war. Parker stood with his hands clasped behind his back, his feet slightly apart, not quite parade-rest, but not quite at attention either. He knew he looked alert, and sometimes that was enough to give him authority.

"*Monsieur.*"

A formerly fat man scrambled down the narrow corridor. His clothes were baggy and so was his skin. The war had taken a toll on him as well. He had sweat on his forehead and his eyes were wild.

"I am Gustav LeRoi. I am in charge of this—how do you say?—operation? Facility?" He waved a pale hand "This place, yes?"

"Yes," Parker said.

"Francois tells me you speak French, but I assume you prefer the English, no?"

"Either is fine," Parker said. "If you are uncertain of your English, we may speak French."

He was being formal partly because the French expected it, but partly because he was going to make a request. He didn't want to be considered obnoxious in any way.

"English is fine," the man said with a hint of a smile, "if you do not mind the occasional lapse into French because of my vocabulary."

"I don't mind," Parker said. "Is there somewhere we may talk in private?"

"*Oui*," LeRoi said. "My office, *s'il vous plaît*."

Then without waiting, he scurried back down that hallway.

The building got noticeably hotter and the metallic smell grew stronger. But the hall was strangely silent. Parker had been in a telephone exchange in the United Kingdom while on a different mission during the war, and that exchange had been anything but quiet—people speaking all the time, over each other, around each other, through each other. He hadn't liked that either, and wondered how someone could work in such chaos.

But he saw no chaos here.

LeRoi's office was at the end of the hallway. LeRoi swept open a heavy wooden door and revealed a wall of windows. Parker had never seen anything quite like it inside a building before.

He walked past the desk and chairs to the windows. They looked down a floor at the exchange itself.

Row after row of women sat on small chairs, thick legs crossed at the ankles, large headsets on their ears. They spoke into microphones, and leaned forward as they stuck metal-tipped prongs into an electronic board in front of them.

Each row had its own electronic board that seemed to go on for miles. The backs of the chairs were far enough away from the back of the board so that the women in the next row wouldn't accidentally hit it. Cables covered with engineer's tape snaked along the floor, looking like a hazard for any woman wearing high heels—which was all of them.

The windows themselves gave off heat, and that metallic stench was stronger here. Parker wondered how LeRoi could work here, in the heat and the smell, but knew that was one question he didn't want to ask.

"They told us this office was temporary," LeRoi said. "They told us we would have a new office by now, but of course we do not. I do not think we will until the government builds us something, but now they tell us they have no money, so we must continue here. As you can see, it is dangerous. We lose power whenever the heat gets too high, and we do not have funds to cool the air."

Parker didn't turn around, but he could see LeRoi reflected in the glass. LeRoi had removed a handkerchief from his pocket and was dabbing at his forehead.

He was nervous and uncomfortable, and it took Parker a moment to understand why. LeRoi hoped that the Americans would help him with his dilemma.

Parker was bound to disappoint him. So he needed to take control of the conversation quickly. "You have heard about the international tribunal the Allies will hold to try war criminals?"

He turned, making the movement military in its precision.

A frown creased LeRoi's sweat-stained forehead. "I have heard of it."

His tone said he thought it a bad idea. Many people did, believing that the Tribunal would simply be an excuse for executions. Most people—at least those Parker talked with—did not believe they needed an excuse to execute the war criminals; the heinousness of the war itself had been crime enough.

"I have been commissioned to find translators," Parker said. "I was told that the best translators in France work here."

LeRoi's frown deepened for just a moment, as he realized that he wouldn't be getting any funds to help him move to a better facility. Then the flattery got through.

"We have excellent translators," he said. "We need that. They must speak several languages and do so well."

"I would like to interview your very best," Parker said.

"And then you will take them from me, no?"

"If they can do the job," Parker said.

LeRoi's shoulders stiffened. "They can," he said, sounding somewhat offended.

"It's an unusual type of translation," Parker said, and then he explained the simultaneous translation system.

"It is impossible," LeRoi said.

"I thought so too," Parker said. "But I can do it, and so can others. That's why I need people used to thinking in a variety of languages, people who are flexible, and quick on their feet."

He wasn't sure if LeRoi understood the idiom, but LeRoi nodded. "We require it of our employees."

"Then, if you don't mind, I would like to interview some of them," Parker said.

"Will we be compensated for the loss of their services?" LeRoi asked.

Parker's gaze met his. Parker couldn't lie, but he wanted to.

"I'm sorry, no," he said. "But I will inform General Eisenhower's staff about your troubles here. It doesn't seem right that such an important connection in the telephone system operates in such difficult conditions."

"*Merci, Monsieur*," LeRoi said with a slight bow. "I shall find you our best."

And with that, he shuttled out the door.

Parker stared after him, having the odd feeling that he had just been played. Then he shook the feeling away, and turned toward the window again.

Rows and rows of women.

He wondered why there were no men.

5

LeRoi quickly prepared a list of a dozen prospective translators. Parker asked for and got a different location to conduct the interviews. He was afraid he would get light-headed within an hour in that room.

Like so many buildings in Paris, the Telephone Exchange shared an enclosed garden with neighboring buildings. Two trees—not quite as tall as the buildings themselves—provided ample shade, and after the heat of that office, the outdoors felt cool.

Parker brought two wooden chairs from inside, and used a wrought iron garden table to take notes. LeRoi actually brought him files on all of the employees, and Parker took time to peruse them before each interview.

Most of the interviews were short. First he asked the women if they were able to leave Paris for an extended stay elsewhere. If they said no, he would send them back inside. He didn't want them changing their minds when they heard the salary. He had had trouble with that be-fore—someone enticed by American money, but so torn by duties back home as to be ineffective. He wanted the problems out of the way immediately.

Once he'd established that a woman was able to leave Paris, he then eased into the actual interview. He was flu-ent in French, Spanish, German, and Italian. He under-stood a smattering of Russian, and he had a few other languages as well.

He would find out what a woman's linguistic exper-tise was, and conduct the interview in that language if he could, switching to French midway through, then switch-ing back again. If the woman could handle the rapid changes, then he asked her to name ten trees, ten automo-bile parts, ten agricultural implements, and ten scientific terms in her specialty language.

The requests always brought the woman up short, and she would ask why. He would explain patiently that it wasn't enough to know the general workings of the other language; she would need to know specialized terms as well.

Women at the exchange knew a lot of social language, but didn't have a lot of technical knowledge—in automo-biles or engineering or agriculture. He was able to dismiss even more right there.

By the end of the day, he had only two candidates, when LeRoi sent the last.

She stepped into the garden as if she owned it. Parker's breath caught.

It was the woman he had seen getting off the Metro the day before.

She wore the same skirt, but this afternoon her blouse was white, setting off her skin. Her eyes, which he hadn't been able to see the day before, were so black they matched her hair.

And she had that luminescence, as if she had swallowed a piece of the sun.

She was even more beautiful than he remembered. His heart was pounding as he asked her to sit down.

She carried gloves, which he found odd, given the heat. Then he remembered the notation that had fallen out of her file when he picked it up. She would work in the Phone Exchange only on the condition that she could wear gloves while touching the equipment.

Apparently the Phone Exchange had said yes.

She smiled ever so softly, gathered her skirt around her legs and eased gracefully into the chair. He watched her, something he had not done with the others. With them, he had examined their files as they settled into the chair, but he didn't dare touch hers. If he did, she would notice that his hands were shaking.

Besides, the file didn't tell him much. He had seen files like that before during the war. The application she had filled out for the job left out much of the requested information, including date of birth and the names of her parents.

Because she made him nervous, he decided he would throw her off-balance right from the start.

"Mademoiselle Nathalie Renard," he said, carefully pronouncing her first name so that she could hear the soft "th," "that is your real name?"

"Yes, Monsieur," she said.

"Really? You expect me to believe that your name is Natalie the Fox?"

He said her first name in the American fashion the second time.

She looked at him, her expression guarded.

"You do know that 'fox' has many meanings in English," he said. "Particularly American slang."

Her fingertips brushed the edge of her file as she folded her hands. She almost set them on the top of the table, but she paused without touching it, then moved away from it as if it were wet.

"You do not find me beautiful then?" she asked with a slight smile. "I am not a fox?"

Her accent was heavy, very French and very seductive. He did find her beautiful, but he wasn't about to tell her.

"I think you believe you are as sly as a fox, Mademoiselle, but your file begs to differ. It tells me that you have a past you do not want to reveal."

"Don't we all?" she asked as if she knew his.

"Did you collaborate?" he asked in very sharp German, his accent deliberately Prussian and harsh.

"Of course not," she said in the same language. There was not a trace of France in her voice.

"I suppose you would have me believe you were in the Resistance," he said in French.

"I do not care what you believe," she said in French.

"What did you do during the war, Signorina *Fox*?" he asked in Italian this time, all except for the word "fox" which he kept in English.

"I worked here," she answered in the same language. "You may ask Signore LeRoi."

"Your file says you got your job here in 1943," he said in Spanish. "What did you do before that?"

"I searched for, found, and mourned my family," she said, her Spanish filled with the lisps of Madrid.

She said that to shame him, and it would have worked as recently as a few years before. But he no longer had shame. He had learned that even the most innocent-looking people lied, and lied about terrible things.

Besides, she wasn't the only one who had lost or buried someone. If he asked anyone—anyone at all—in that phone exchange, he would learn that most of them had lost family. And all of them had lost someone close.

"I see," he said. "You mourned your family."

She stiffened just enough for him to notice.

"Then why aren't they mentioned in your files? You don't even give your parents' names in the space provided for it."

Her gaze went flat and for a moment, her eyes elongated, the irises covering the whites. Then she blinked, and they looked normal again.

He hadn't moved. It had been a trick of the light, nothing more. And not the light that seemed to come from her. The dappled sunlight coming through the leaves on the tree above him.

"I was born in Germany," she said in German so heavily accented that he almost didn't understand it. The accent was German—he knew that much. Each region of Germany had its own accent, but he didn't recognize this one. "My family died in the camps."

He was concentrating so hard on the obscure accent that he nearly missed what she had said.

"You're Jewish?" he asked in English. He couldn't quite keep the surprise from his voice.

"It wasn't only Jews that went to the camps," she said in that same odd German. He struggled to understand her. He concentrated on that, again, and it took a moment to realize that she still hadn't answered his question.

"What is your real name?" he asked in his Prussian-accented German, figuring she had the best chance of following a command given to her in that language.

"Nathalie Renard," she said, returning to her French accent.

"That is not a German name," he said, still using his German.

"Yet it is my legal name," she said in French. "You may check if you like."

She handed him her papers. They had been stamped by the French government. They did not list her religion on them, as the Nazis had required. Nor did they list a place of birth, although there was a space supplied for that.

The lack of information wasn't as unusual as Parker made it sound. But generally it was older people who didn't have the correct information, because the record-keeping was poor or because the government couldn't verify the information. Not, usually, with a woman as young as Renard.

He handed her papers back to her, and tried not to sigh. She had gone with him on a linguistic journey that put the others he had tested to shame. Her accent in every language—except for (including?) that odd German—was flawless.

"Give me the name of ten different trees in English, please," he said in that language, beginning her tests.

"Birch," she said, surprising him. Most started with oak or elm, primarily because they had learned the tree names as street names. She gave the names of nine other trees, then asked, "Does this mean I'm hired?"

"No," he said, and then he realized he had skipped a step. "In fact, you may not want the work, considering what happened to your family. I am looking for translators for the International Tribunal. You will hear testimony about the treatment of prisoners in the camps. What happened there is not…."

He was going to say "pretty" but the word did not belong in the same sentence as those camps.

"What happened there is appalling," he said. "You may not want to know."

"I already know," she said softly.

He nodded. Of course she did, if her story about her family was true.

"If we chose you to help," he said, "you would have to go to Nuremberg. Maybe for six months."

"Nürnberg," she said, using the German pronunciation. He wasn't sure, but it seemed as if she had grown a bit pale. "For six months?"

"Is that possible?" he asked.

"I have no ties here," she said. "I have a job."

He waited, but she said no more. He took that as a yes.

"You will discuss trees at this trial?" she asked. The question seemed almost like an attempt at levity, and with anyone else, he would have thought that was exactly what it was. But it wasn't. She was actually curious.

"We will discuss everything at this trial," he said, and left it at that.

She tilted her head and looked at him sideways out of those almond-shaped eyes.

He felt cold suddenly, despite the heat of the afternoon. Her eyes were flat. They had no light in them at all, which was odd, since he only thought of light when he saw her.

"And who will be on trial here?" she asked. "Whose words will I have to translate?"

It was a valid question. At that moment, he realized he hadn't told her much of anything about the trial. He certainly hadn't given his speech, the one he had been giving all the others he interviewed, the one about leaving Paris for an extended stay, about the fact that even if they go to Nuremberg, they might not test well there, and have to return. He hadn't told her much of anything.

"The Tribunal is still drawing up the names for the indictment," he said.

"Surely, you have an inkling," she said.

He frowned. "Does it matter?"

"Your newspapers here, they say this will be a trial, justice, the rule of law." She spoke with great sarcasm. "It will restore order into this chaotic world, show that we are civilized people. Isn't that what your Robert Jackson is saying?"

She knew more about this than he expected, and he didn't like it. She was still staring at him with her head tilted sideways, her eyes flat. He felt like a mouse, trapped by a fox, and the fox was about to spring.

"The Nazis didn't not believe in the law—"

"You do not have to tell me about Nazis," she snapped. "I am quite familiar with them."

He raised his chin. With that outburst, it felt like the interview had gone back into his control.

"So you did collaborate," he said.

"I did *not*," she said. "I would not. I am insulted by this continual assumption that everyone who stayed in France did so by lying on their backs and letting the Nazis do whatever they wanted."

"Isn't that what you did?" he asked.

"*I* did not do that," she said.

"So you were in the Resistance," he said.

"No," she said, surprising him. He thought everyone had been in the Resistance. That's what they all said. No one had acquiesced. Others had, but not the people he talked to. Even when their own personal record made it clear that they couldn't have been part of the Resistance, they still claimed it. They wanted to believe it themselves.

"What did you do, then?" he asked.

"I answered the phone," she said.

"I thought you searched for your parents," he said.

"I did," she said. "I mourned them."

"You said that before. For all your languages, you aren't very precise."

She gave him that flat look again, then leaned away from him, and rested her elbow on the back of her chair. She made herself seem relaxed, and he knew she wasn't. No more than he was.

"Your trial," she said. "It is a show trial. You will execute the defendants when you're done, no matter what they say. You will let none of them go."

"You say that as if it is a fact," he said.

"What is the point, otherwise? It is just a way to put— how do you say it in America?—window-dressing on the occasion. You will put these men on trial, and then you will kill them, and you will spend money and time so that you can prove the rule of law is back when it is not. It will be the same as always. The victors have made up their minds, and they will make everyone else see how right they are, before the scheduled executions."

He shook his head. "We're not doing that."

"You do not need to bring the world to your opinion," she said as if he hadn't spoken. "The world already agrees. Why do you not execute them now? Save time, save money? Hmm? It makes more sense."

He was still shaking his head. "We don't do that. We don't prejudge. We need fairness."

"You do?" she asked. "Why? It is ridiculous, this 'fairness' of yours. I have never understood it. It makes no sense. These men have ruined the world, murdered millions. They deserve death. And, I say, they deserve a long, horrible death, one in which they suffer mightily."

Her eyes flashed now with light, so much light that it almost hurt. Her words were violent, filled with power. He could feel the force of them, hitting him as if each word was a tiny knife.

"I don't disagree with that," he said quietly. "But I am not making the decisions."

"Why do you work for those who do?" she asked.

He stared at her, unable to answer, because if he answered, he would tell her about the drive back from the camps. He was supposed to get support staff, to find trucks and vans and medical personnel to help the survivors—and he did.

He did.

But not before he saw a German man hiding in a culvert, wearing the tattered remains of a uniform. Clearly, that man had been one of the guards who had fled, and clearly, he hadn't been that bright. Later, Parker learned that many of the guards dressed as prisoners and got into the system as victims. Other guards fled days before and returned home, bundling their uniforms into a ball, leaving them behind, swearing they had worked in their town all along, and getting their friends and family—those who were left—to swear the same thing.

But this man had not. He had gotten lost or he had had second thoughts or maybe he had stayed to close the camps. Some stayed to burn the camps and never quite managed it.

It didn't matter who the man was or what he had done, because Parker had gotten out of his Jeep, pointed his rifle at the man and told him, in German, to stand. The man hadn't moved. Parker repeated the command, stronger, and the man rose.

Parker's partner, Mark McGuilicuty, said softly, "We need to take him prisoner."

"I'm not in the mood to take prisoners," Parker said, and shot the German.

Not once, not twice, but more times than he could think. More times than he wanted to think about.

They left the corpse beside the road, and Parker had no idea what happened to it. He did know that the death was not part of his official report. Nor was it part of Mc-Guilicuty's report. No one knew.

Except McGuilicuty, and he wasn't telling.

Parker certainly wasn't going to mention this to Nathalie Renard, not now. Not ever.

"You ask why I work for them," he said softly. "I work for them because I want to believe they're right."

She crossed her arms, then sighed. She clearly did not agree, but she was just as clearly done arguing with him. She did not respond.

After a moment, he said, "Now that you know what the work is and what it's for, I take it you're not interested."

"What are you paying?" she asked.

He hadn't answered that question for anyone else. Most were too polite to ask. "We haven't finished the testing," he said. "I don't know if you'll be qualified for the work."

But he lied. He hadn't heard such facility with language from anyone else he tested. He suspected that she would know all the strange quirks of language, from names of agricultural implements to scientific terms.

She gave him a cold smile. He suddenly understood the phrase "terrifyingly beautiful." He had always believed it poetic license before.

"You do not want me after all," she said.

"It'll be hard," he said. "And you'll have to give it everything."

"I can do that," she said.

"Even though you don't believe in the mission?" He used the military term on purpose. Because it was a military endeavor, for all the civilians involved. Or at least it was for him. He was following orders.

Orders always worked when belief itself was difficult.

"I would simply translate one person's words into another person's language, would I not?" she asked.

"You would be working hard," he said.

"I do not dispute that. But it is not my views on trial, is it?" she said.

"We would have to trust you," he said. "We need to believe you will translate accurately."

Her cheeks flushed and for a moment, he wondered if he had insulted her. "Be truthful," she said. "If I had not spoken up about the meaning of your trial, would you be offering me the work?"

"Can you name ten truck parts in German?" he asked.

She recited the names of the equipment in German, as if the very question offended her. Then she added the same names in Russian, Czech, French, Spanish, and—

"Enough," he said, holding up his hand. She was right; if she hadn't spoken up about the trial he would be begging her to come.

He sighed. "You would be in Germany for more than six months. You would still need to be going through tests there, but that's to see where you would be placed."

Because he couldn't imagine anyone turning her down. Normally, he warned the potential translators that they might come to Nuremberg only to go home again on the next train.

"You would be hired by the American military, so you would receive payment according to our pay sheets. We would pay in dollars, but I'm told that our paymasters can work with your bank, so that half of the funds would be deposited here."

He hadn't said that to anyone on this trip. He hadn't needed to. Usually someone else gave that speech at the official hire in Nuremberg itself.

She nodded once, then gave him a grim smile.

"I am not sure I want to be part of your show trial," she said. "I would like time to think about it."

"I'll be here tomorrow, finishing up," he said. "I can give you the documents that will get you to Nuremberg then."

"All right," she said, and stood up.

He stood too. It was his training.

She slipped away from the table without another word, without looking at him. He watched her walk to the main door. He waited until she had gone inside before sitting back down.

She was, by far, the best candidate he had ever seen. He wasn't sure how many languages she spoke fluently; it seemed like every time he made a request, she added a new one.

The Tribunal needed someone like that, someone who could float from position to position, handling whatever came up.

But he hadn't liked the look on her face when he mentioned accuracy—not because he doubted she could be accurate, but because he wondered if she would even try.

Then he shook off the discomfort she had aroused in him, sat down, and went back to work.

6

NONE OF THE OTHER CANDIDATES MEASURED UP. How could they? Not only was she amazingly talented, but she was beautiful.

And she had challenged him.

He couldn't stop thinking about her, even though he tried. After he was done, he found the bar that the Army preferred and drank with some new friends. But that didn't clear her from his mind. Neither did the exceptionally long dinner at a restaurant that had been a favorite of the Germans. Most of the remaining restaurants in Paris had been favorites of the Germans. The other restaurants had been closed or burned or destroyed, and since the war ended, no one had the money to start something new.

Everything was a compromise, even the place where he had food. He thought that, realized he was still arguing with her in his head, and tried to stop. But he couldn't stop. He mentally argued with her in his hotel—which the

Nazis had used to bunk their highest ranking officers, in Paris on a visit. He finally managed to quell the argument enough to sleep, but only with a promise that he would talk with her again in the morning.

He went to the Phone Exchange and she never showed up.

He interviewed the remaining candidates, selected four of them, and then spoke to LeRoi, who said she didn't have a shift that day. Nor did she have a phone—which, although it was ironic, wasn't that uncommon after the war. Even party lines were too expensive. Everyone was saving money somehow.

She had decided not to support the Tribunal, and part of him was relieved about that. He had meant what he said about trust.

But part of him wanted to continue the discussion. Part of him wanted to argue with her and flirt with her, and get to know her better.

Even with her terrible, terrible beauty.

7

HE ARRIVED IN NUREMBERG IN MID-SEPTEMBER, WEARY and spent. He had traveled all over Europe, finding translators, arguing with professors of language, nearly getting tossed out of the League of Nations building in Geneva for arguing against consecutive translation.

As if he had had a choice. Shortly after he had left Paris, he learned that the Tribunal had decided to run simultaneous translation. He also learned that they had decided to use the Anglo-American adversarial legal system, with its talk-heavy jurisprudence. Witness examination would be relatively easy to translate, but cross-examination would test the system to its limits.

Plus, the Tribunal insisted on accuracy. He was informed that he would need people who could take shorthand in the various languages as well.

He had found them. He had found a lot of people and sent them ahead to Nuremberg. Most of them stayed, not to do simultaneous translation, but to translate documents. On his last phone call with Alfred Steer, the Deputy Chief of the Translation Division, Parker learned that he would be one of the main English to German simultaneous translators in addition to all of the other duties the Tribunal planned to assign him.

He had too much time to think about that. It had taken him two days to get to the city because he had traveled by train. And the trains no longer ran on time. Sometimes, they didn't run at all.

Germany was not the country he had seen before the war. Every city had bomb damage, and some cities were completely destroyed. The Allies had fixed some train tracks but not all.

Everywhere he went, he saw people on foot—either walking to their home city or walking away from somewhere else. The air stank of rot, and the once-orderly countryside was littered with abandoned vehicles, abandoned goods, and abandoned people.

It got so that he did not look out the train windows. He either slept or read, although he could not read fiction. Made-up worlds with their fake order and their perfect endings had no meaning for him. He couldn't escape into them.

He couldn't escape at all.

He read newspapers or briefing documents, and tried hard not to think of what was ahead.

What was ahead was another devastated city, this one nearly flattened by bombs earlier in the year. The train station was a burned-out shell, with only a few platforms.

His instructions were simple: once he arrived, he checked in at Army Headquarters, and then went to his billet.

Army Headquarters was at the Palace of Justice where the Tribunal would be held. It turned out that the Palace of Justice was a few miles from the train station, but the Grand Hotel, where he was going to be billeted, was supposed to be across the street.

He decided to go to the hotel first.

If he could find it.

Nuremberg was not the city he had visited before the war. It was a pile of ruins, worse than anything he had seen on his travels. When he had been here before, he had come out of the train station, looked up the hill and saw the Nuremberg Imperial Castle, towering over the city.

Now when he looked up, he saw rubble, and above it, a single burned out tower that might or might not have been the castle. And as he looked, he had no idea how to get up there, because most of the streets were not clear.

The stench was awful. Clearly, there were still bodies in the ruins.

He shifted his duffel from one shoulder to the other. The best hotels in Nuremberg had been near the train station, but when he was here in the thirties, he hadn't stayed in an expensive hotel. He knew that Hitler had preferred the Hotel Deutscher Hof, and that it was somewhere near the Grand Hotel. But in those days, every hotel had hung the Nazi flag outside, and every hotel had seemed like a place that housed Nazis.

He had avoided them, even then.

He stared at the ruins, uncertain how to find anything. Finally, a man in a British military uniform got out of a town car. Parker walked over to him.

"Excuse me," he said. "Where's the Grand Hotel?"

"Over there, mate." The man pointed kitty-corner across the street.

There a five-story building dominated the block. So much scaffolding covered the exterior that Parker hadn't even realized the building was one of the hotels. When he peered at it, he saw the elegant design from the turn of the century, and remembered how spectacular the hotel had looked ten years before.

Now the building was covered with soot and fire damage, but the brown stone façade seemed sturdy enough. The upper level windows were gone, replaced with brick. In front of the entrance, two military guards stood, which should have been his clue that the hotel had been commandeered by the Tribunal.

He thanked the British soldier, then crossed the street, careful not to trip in holes in the cobblestone. The rubble had been removed here, but the street was still treacherous. Fortunately, there weren't a lot of vehicles going by. He made it to the sidewalk, and walked around to an awning covered double-entrance.

Military police stood at attention in front of the door. They nodded at him as he went inside.

The building was cool. He blinked in the artificial light. He couldn't tell if the hotel had an odor all its own; his nostrils were still filled with the stench of death from the streets.

It felt like he had suddenly stepped from destruction to civilization. A red and gold carpet ran along the center of the marble floor, urging him toward two long stairs. Near the windows, men in uniform sat in round chairs, smoking, and drinking coffee. Some sat alone, reading *The Stars and Stripes*, others conversed softly in the kind of tone he hadn't heard in years.

He cast about for some kind of front desk. To his left, a bar full of patrons despite the early hour, and to his right, a restaurant that had a rope across the opening, with a sign announcing dinner service would begin at six sharp.

"Looking for someone?"

He turned. A black-haired man in rumpled Army green stood near the door, a wide grin on his face. Mark McGuilicuty.

Parker hadn't expected to see him here.

"Mac," Parker said. "I thought you were heading home."

Mac shrugged. "Home sounded like a good idea, but there wasn't much to go back to."

"What happened to Judy?"

"She found a new guy," Mac said. "Got the divorce papers special delivery. The week after you left. Nice, huh."

The week after Parker left. The week after they had gone to the camps.

"I'm sorry," Parker said.

"Naw," Mac said. "It was one of those wartime marriages. God knows what'd've been when I got home and we actually had to talk instead of screwing each other blind."

Parker laughed, but only because he was supposed to. Then he extended his hand. "Good to see you, my friend."

Mac took it, shook hard, then grinned. "Good to see you too. I didn't expect you until next week. What'd you do, fly across the continent?"

"It didn't seem that way," Parker said. "And why were you expecting me?"

"I'm the meet, greet, and dump committee," Mac said. "Today I was dumping. I sent off a big load of terrible translators back to their little home towns."

Parker felt his face warm. "Some of those translators mine?"

"I have no idea who sent them here," Mac said. "I just get to deliver them to the train station when they wash out. Most of them take one look at this place and deliberately start talking gibberish. I mean, who would stay?"

Parker frowned. The hotel didn't seem that bad. In fact, it seemed nice, considering. But he didn't say that.

"I guess I was supposed to show up here," he said.

"Yep," Mac said. "You get to billet here until they decide what to do with you. C'mon over to reception, such as it is."

He led Parker across the carpet to the long wooden desk which had actually been polished. The illusion of an old hotel got lost, however, when Mac got behind the desk and searched through the reservations book.

"There you are," he said. He turned, grabbed a key, and then dangled it near Parker. "This is not a regular hotel, you know."

"I figured," Parker said.

"No room service—of any kind. No females on your floor, no exception. No linen service, no nothing. Treat this like your camp bunk and keep it neat. You got that?"

"I got it," Parker said.

"Okay. Your food is covered, but drinks are not. The restaurant over there— " and he waggled his hand toward a side door "— is not part of the food allowance. You'll be eating back there."

He waved a hand toward the darkness.

"And you'll be there at six or you'll miss your meal. Got that?"

Parker nodded.

Mac dropped the key into Parker's hand. "I'll be back at 0800 to pick you up and take you to the Palace of Justice. Expect to work long and hard tomorrow."

"What about today?" Parker asked. "There's still a lot of daylight left."

"You got that right. But you're lucky. No one expected you today. So get some rest. It'll probably be your last chance until April."

When, theoretically, the trial would be over.

Parker nodded. "Anything I need to know?"

Mac's expression hardened. "Take a good look at the carpet, my friend. Then ask yourself 'What the hell are we doing here?' Because I'm not sure I get it. Maybe you will."

Parker glanced down. The carpet, faded and scuffed, but its swastika pattern was still clearly visible. He nodded. So Mac felt the same way he had. It didn't feel so much like they had conquered the Nazis as it felt as if they had stepped into their lives.

He looked up at Mac. Mac's expression was cool now, as if he was thinking about that last time they had seen each other. Parker gave him a regretful smile, then shook his head.

"It is good to see you," he said.

"Yeah," Mac said. "Strangely enough, it's good to see you too."

8

PARKER'S ROOM WAS ON THE ALL-MALE THIRD FLOOR.
The corridors were wide and plush, the rooms themselves
a revelation, with an attached bathroom and a bed big
enough to sleep three. For the moment, Parker roomed
alone, although he suspected he'd have a roommate before
the trial was over.

He thought he'd get some rest, but he learned quickly
that the Grand Hotel was not a restful place to stay. Instead, it was a bastion of frenetic gaiety, the kind that
came from people who were increasingly desperate. In
addition to the bar he saw when he came in, the hotel had
two others, one so exclusive that only VIPs were allowed
inside—and that did not include him.

At night, different jazz bands entertained. Drinking
and dancing went on into the wee hours, and if anyone
paid attention to the non-fraternization rule, Parker didn't
know who that was.

He tried not to pay attention to the debauchery around him. He had more duties than he knew how to handle. He was setting up the document translation unit as well as training the new simultaneous interpretation staff. He was also one of the people Dostert brought in to test the newcomers, who seemed to arrive in the dozens every single day.

For some, this trial was a holy mission, a way of shedding the horrors of the past by punishing the ones who caused them. For others, it was a duty. Most, however, didn't talk about it, and he had no idea why they were there.

In fact, he hadn't talked about the purpose of the Tribunal with anyone since he had spoken to the intriguing Nathalie Renard in Paris. And that seemed like years ago.

It was not years. Just weeks. But it felt as if he had been in Nuremberg for half of his life.

The Palace of Justice was outside the Old City, and had been built thirty years before, a big Neo-Renaissance building that took up an entire city block by itself. It was part of a larger complex, apparently built by the Bavarian government before the Great War, and attached to the nearly 100-year-old prison where the defendants were being held.

A five-million dollar renovation was underway, repairing the ruined roof and some of the destroyed upper floors. If it weren't for the smell of sawdust and the sight of construction workers, the Palace of Justice would seem relatively normal.

But the walk he took every day to the Palace of Justice was anything but normal. He preferred to walk, even in the rain, because it allowed him some time alone.

He watched the city as it tried to recover. Former Nazi officials—lower level, not worth arresting—were assigned tasks like rubble removal. Anyone who complained dealt with the corpses, still buried in the debris six months after the bombings.

The Germans, as General Eisenhower reminded anyone who asked him, were a *conquered* people. They never surrendered. As a result, they were all possible combatants and all considered criminal.

Even the starving children that Parker saw on his walk. He had gathered quite a crowd of them day to day. He wasn't supposed to interact with the locals at all, but he gave what he could to those children—apples, candy bars, cigarettes. The cigarettes could be traded for food; the locals' daily food allotment was so small that a black market economy had sprung up. Locals traded goods, services, antiques—anything they could—for something to eat.

He hated it. He hated it all.

But he wouldn't help the adults. He couldn't.

Those adults, they had known. No matter what they said, they had known.

He liked the fact that he wasn't supposed to interact with them. Because he wasn't sure what he would say.

Fortunately, he didn't have to go with the lawyers to interrogate the defendants. He almost never saw them.

They were the reason for his work here, but until the trial started, he wouldn't have to interact with them.

They were the worst of the worst, the highest ranking Nazis that the Allies had been able to find. From Hermann Göring to Albert Speer, from Julius Streicher to Rudolph Hess, these were men who had believed—no, more than believed, who had *devised* National Socialism and all of its evils.

Hitler wasn't here because he had killed himself. So had Goebbels, along with his entire family. It almost felt like a cheat. What had Nathalie Renard said? *They deserve a long, horrible death, one in which they suffer mightily.*

Hitler, Goebbels, so many of the others, they had cheated the Allies of that death. And sometimes, Parker wondered if this Tribunal wasn't cheating as well.

Particularly when one after another, his translators refused to go into the prison wing. They could not stomach the defendants.

Parker learned that in his first week, when one young American—Rueben White—stumbled his way back to the translation unit. His eyes were red-rimmed, his lips chapped. He found Parker, who was trying to figure out how anyone was going to monitor the Russian documents, and pulled him aside.

"I need to go to my room," White said. He had been recruited by the Washington D.C. team. He was twenty-one, and had been unable to serve in the military because he was 4F, but he had volunteered to come here, use the German he had learned at home to expiate his guilt at remaining in college while his friends went off to war.

The translation unit got a lot of applications from young men like him, but hadn't taken most of them. White, a first-generation American, was an exception. His German was flawless, and his attitude, until that afternoon, upbeat.

"Something happen?" Parker asked, not because he cared—he didn't want to be these people's confessor; there were military chaplains for that—but because he needed to know if these people could work. Besides, if he was telling himself the truth, he liked White. The kid had been one of the translation unit's early rocks.

White's lower lip trembled. Parker thought he was going to burst into tears, but somehow White managed to maintain control.

"These *fuckers*," he said, and the word burst out of him as if he had been trying to hold it back along with his tears. "They don't care about anyone. They think what they did is right and they're trying to cover it up only because they're in our custody, but the way they look at you when you're talking to them—God."

Parker put a hand on his shoulder. White was trembling.

"You know the worst of it?" he asked. "They look at me like I *understand*."

He took one sideways step so Parker's hand was no longer on his shoulder.

"Respectfully, I'd like to go back to my room, sir. I need a shower."

Parker nodded. "Take the day."

He would have liked to give White the next day as well, but they didn't have the next day. They were still short dozens of translators.

White nodded, and left. Parker sighed and reached for the roster, to see who White had been translating for. Parker's hand stopped in mid-air.

He didn't want to know. Couldn't know, really. Because whatever the defendants were telling the lawyers was nothing compared with the testimony everyone would hear at the trial. Right now, the defendants were giving depositions, trying to dismantle a case, trying to minimize.

They wouldn't be able to minimize photographs and films.

And the survivors.

But Parker did make a mental note: Only the strongest of his translators would work the toughest cases.

9

SOMETIMES HE WASN'T SURE HE WAS STRONG ENOUGH either. He had initially planned to move from the Grand Hotel to a residence. Then he found out he would be rooming with other translators, lawyers, and witnesses, some unindicted (as yet) members of the German High Command.

His hotel room provided a measure of privacy. So far, he didn't have to share, and even if he did get a roommate, it would be someone from the military. If he didn't like the company at the hotel, he didn't have to eat with them like he would have in a house. He didn't have to share a bathroom. He didn't have to pass them on the stairs.

He didn't have to interact if he didn't want to.

And he didn't want to.

He was having enough trouble interacting at the job itself.

The days passed in snapshots—moments when he came to himself. He tried not to think about anything, just work, translate, organize. He had little sleep, but he found that didn't matter. Despite the privacy of his hotel room, sleep usually eluded him.

Sometimes, he thought, he was still arguing with her.

So when he saw her in the corridors of the Palace of Justice, he thought he was imagining her. Nathalie Renard walked past him, up the steps to Courtroom 600, the place where the trial would be held.

Dozens of workers toiled around the clock to finish that courtroom. It was too small for one thing, so they were taking out a back wall. They were also trying to repair bomb damage, and shore up the building.

The architect assigned by the U.S. Military, Dan Kiley, had been told to make the courtroom a showplace, a word that made Parker wince, because of its echoes to Nathalie Renard's remarks. But, Kiley had said over drinks in the Grand Hotel, both President Truman and General Eisenhower believed that press from around the world would cover this trial, and they wanted the courtroom to look as official as possible.

They had removed the furniture, added side rooms for cameras, and had removed all of the Germanic heraldic decorations. They needed so many workers, they had hired a crew from Nuremberg itself without really vetting them, except for their craftsman skills. They needed men who could handle fine work as well as standard carpentry, and they decided to take them as they found them.

Which meant that in addition to the workers, the military needed guards. Sometimes there were as many as fifty people in that room, doing a wide variety of work. And always, no matter how late it was when Parker left, there were at least a dozen, struggling to complete some task.

He was always struggling to complete some task as well, and since he was sleep deprived, seeing Nathalie Renard walk those stairs didn't surprise him as much as it should have. The Tribunal had hired hundreds of women, from nurses to secretaries to translators, and he could have seen anyone of them. It wasn't unusual to see a dark-haired woman in a pale blouse and a black skirt that showed off phenomenal legs. He had seen a lot of good-looking women here, and had he been in a better frame of mind, he would have ignored the non-fraternizaton rule.

But he hadn't. It was easier to focus on the work.

So he ignored the woman and went into the translation division's office.

Office was the wrong word. He worked in a room with dozens of others. Papers were scattered everywhere, including on the floor. He moved from desk to desk, table to table, answering questions, organizing, getting work done.

He was supervising the translations of yet another cache of German documents that one of the prosecutors needed for the trial. The documents were discouraging, chilling in their efficiency: the trains moving Jews and gypsies and "enemies of the Reich" to the camps. The numbers totaling everything, from the number of people transported to the number killed to the number of corpses burned in various ovens. The ages of the victims—from less than a year to more than ninety. The experiments performed on the living. The amount of gold found in teeth pulled before death.

Occasionally, he had to stop, look away, force himself to blink. He couldn't scrub his mind of the images from the camps, and now he couldn't scrub his mind of the cold method in which those camps came about.

He stepped outside the room for just a minute, trying to get air. The corridors were cooler than the rooms, partly because of the high ceilings, and partly because of the wide design. Benches were staggered every few feet.

He studied them as if they were as important as the documents. They gave his mind somewhere to rest.

Then he heard footsteps coming up the stairs. There were several disadvantages of the wide stone corridors. The main one was the acoustics. Everything echoed, from the click of heels on marble to whispered conversations.

His shoulders slumped for a moment. Then he took a deep breath, and turned, figuring whoever was in this corridor had come for the translation division.

He was right. One of the other deputies, Lawrence Felton, made his way slowly across the floor.

Felton was in his sixties, career military, wounded in the Great War. He had managed translators for decades, and had excellent organizational skills. He couldn't handle simultaneous translation, partly because he didn't want to, but he seemed to know how to keep translators calm, focused, and on task.

Dostert had assigned him to the Russian delegation because the Russians insisted on finding their own translators, and then with characteristic stubbornness, hadn't brought any to the translation division.

Felton nodded at him as he got close. Parker could hear him breathe, even from a few yards away. Felton had been gassed, and it had burned through his lungs. He had once said it was amazing he could talk at all, let alone talk in more than one language.

Technically, he should have been medically discharged long ago, but he refused and since he had a non-combat role, no one had insisted on his dismissal.

"Good," he said as he stopped next to Parker, "you're here."

Parker almost said *Where else would I be?* but he knew that the sarcasm wouldn't be appreciated. He also knew that this discussion would be about one of two things— the simultaneous translation equipment that was supposed to be delivered the following day, or the Russians' intransigence. He hoped it was about the equipment. Dostert talked of it as if it were a miracle, these boxes and cables all made by some experts at International Business Machines. Parker wasn't sure he believed in miracles. He also wasn't sure what they'd do if the translation equipment didn't work.

"Has it arrived?" he asked, hoping to steer the conversation in the right direction.

"What?" Felton asked, frowning. Then he seemed to understand. "No. No one has heard from the drivers for two days."

Parker didn't hide his disappointment.

"I think we're going to need to hire our own Russian translators. I met with the delegation, and they only acknowledge four. We can't do this work with four."

They couldn't do the work with twenty, and now they were behind.

"We've been ordered not to—"

"How many documents do you have translated into Russian?" Felton asked.

Parker sighed. "Not enough."

"The Russian judge is already complaining about his workload. If he has to read all of the documents at the last minute, then he'll insist on a delay."

The trial's opening had already been delayed once. It had been scheduled to start on the first of November, but by the end of September it had become clear that there was too much work to do in the building to allow that to happen.

"Do you have anyone who can translate the documents?"

"Not here," Parker said.

"Perhaps you should ask in Berlin," said a female voice behind Parker.

In Russian.

He turned, and there she was, for real this time. Nathalie Renard, looking bright and beautiful in the dim light. She wore the same black skirt that she had worn in August, and a blouse, just like he had seen when she climbed the stairs. Her black hair was pulled back into a chignon, accenting the angles of her cheekbones. With her upswept dark eyes and her expression of calm alertness, she actually resembled the fox of her name.

He wondered how she had gotten here, who had approved her, and who had given her the badge pinned to her collar.

"You know this woman?" Felton asked in English, his voice clipped.

"Sir, let me present Mademoiselle Nathalie Renard. She has French citizenship, but she claims to have been born here in Germany." Parker's words sounded abrupt, even to him. But he didn't like the surprise. Nor did he like how close she stood to him or the fact that she had snuck up on him in that echoey hallway.

"Claims?" Felton asked.

"In our interview, she was vague about her origins," Parker said.

"Yet you brought her here," Felton said, with just a hint of disapproval.

"He did not bring me anywhere, Monsieur," Nathalie said in French. "He asked me if I was interested, and I did not answer him. That was in Paris, in August. I wasn't sure if I wanted to come to Germany."

Parker was startled by the lie. It wasn't Germany that provided her hesitation. It was the Tribunal itself.

"And yet, here you are," Parker said in English.

"Here I am," she repeated.

"This seems very irregular," Felton said to Parker.

"It is," Parker said. "But as you can see, she is a gifted linguist."

"We have to be able to trust our translators," Felton said.

Parker nodded. "I'm not sure of the range of her skills. I asked her to come here back in August because I wanted to see if she could handle simultaneous translation. Before we make any decisions about her, we will need to test her."

"She is right here," Nathalie said, "and she does speak fluent English."

"I am sorry, Mademoiselle," Felton said in French, "but this was a private conversation long before you arrived."

She raised her eyebrows slightly, then looked at Parker as if gauging his reaction.

He had no idea what his reaction was. She made him nervous, and yet he wanted to stare at her because she was the most beautiful woman he had ever seen. He didn't trust her, but he wanted to touch her, and he knew, somehow, that touching her would be wrong.

"We don't have time to deal with difficult people," Felton said to Parker, "no matter how talented they are."

Then Felton gave Nathalie a pointed glance. She didn't move away.

Felton sighed, and looked back at Parker. "We will leave the Russian issue for now. Tend to your new problem, and I will speak to you later."

Then he clasped his hands behind his back and headed down the hall.

"Touchy," she said.

"People do not show up here unannounced," he said.

She shrugged a shoulder as if that didn't concern her. She started to say something when the entire building groaned.

Suddenly there was a loud crack behind him, followed by crashing. Parker turned, saw dust and debris, then felt the floor move. He lost his footing, saw Nathalie slip and start to slide toward the debris.

He fell forward, landing on her, wrapping his body around hers, then hooked an arm on one of the built-in benches, and hoped it would hold.

The cracking continued, along with crashing and screams. The noise seemed to go on forever.

And then it stopped as suddenly as it started.

Dust so thick that it felt like snow fell around them. Parker coughed, his mouth coated, his eyes scratching. Nathalie moved, sliding sideways just a little so she could peer around him.

The floor was canted downward.

Parker pulled them both forward until the floor felt level again. He turned, wiping at his face. The dust continued to billow.

From below, he heard wailing.

There was a gigantic hole where part of the floor used to be. He leaned, hoping the dust would settle enough so that he could see, but he couldn't.

Then he heard shouts and cries, not of pain or panic this time, but of rescuers jumping into work.

He left Nathalie by the stairs and gingerly made his way to the hole. First he looked up and saw the interior of the courtroom, with its scaffolding and boarded windows.

The floor had collapsed.

He looked down.

It had collapsed all the way to the basement.

The billowing dust rose from there, hiding all but the tallest debris. His heart was pounding. He had to get down there and see what he could do to help.

He didn't dare get near the hole—it was too unstable. Besides, he couldn't climb down, not without dislodging something else.

He ran back to the stairs. Nathalie was still standing there, her face coated in white. Only her eyes peeked out, as if she wore a chalk mask.

"What happened?" she asked, sounding breathless.

"Floor collapsed," he said as he hurried down the stairs. He was joined by several other military personnel, as well as the medical unit from their station inside the building. The farther down he went, the more people seemed to appear out of the dust, running toward the debris.

"Is more going to fall?" a woman asked from behind him.

"No way to know," the guy next to him said.

"That's why we gotta move fast," someone else said.

Parker didn't talk. He just ran. And when he reached the basement, he stopped, startled at the pile of broken boards and shattered marble. Someone was crying nearby, and father away, he heard that semi-conscious moaning only the most severely injured made.

He started pulling boards away. Someone handed him gloves. He looked up, saw one of the nurses. She was giving out the gloves to everyone working, probably wanting to prevent punctures that could cause tetanus. Practical.

They were all practical now, used to crisis. It had been such a part of their lives for so many years.

He pulled out boards and handed them to the man behind him, who passed them to someone else. The boards were stacking up in the back. Occasionally, he'd reach a slab of marble he couldn't lift, and he'd motion for help.

Without him even asking, someone would come over and lift with him. They would move the marble aside and get back to the boards, moving, shifting, digging, until they got to the first victim.

Her left leg was trapped between the remains of a table, but she was working hard to free herself. Her hands were covered in marble dust and blood, her hair loose, her face scratched, but she seemed lucid.

Parker and one of the privates managed to lift the table off her—it was heavy and oak and jammed against something else—then the medical staff pulled her free. Her leg was a mass of blood and tissue, and despite himself, Parker looked away.

He kept digging, finding three more injured victims, all conscious, all able to help.

Then he got to the first dead body.

A worker, by his clothes, not military. Parker couldn't make out his features under the dirt and blood and dust, but he could see the cause of death. The man had been impaled by a long bit of wood.

Parker touched the man's neck just to make sure. But there was no pulse. The man wasn't breathing.

Parker nodded toward the man behind him, then moved forward, letting the others deal with the body. He dug and pulled and moved until his gloves ripped and his back ached.

And then he found the other worker. A man he'd seen in the corridors. He'd actually helped the guy carry a ladder once, and they'd had a slight conversation in German. The man was local, a craftsman who was carving some paneling to replace the original paneling destroyed in the bombing.

"You'll be all right," Parker said in German.

But he wasn't sure if he was telling the truth. The man was coated in blood, his stomach flayed open by something—maybe some of the marble, maybe his own tools. The stench was awful, which meant that his intestines had been punctured.

Parker wasn't sure they had any facilities in Nuremberg that could help a man with a gut torn up that badly.

"The floor," the man said weakly, also speaking German. "It just collapsed."

The building had been unstable, but the engineers thought they had leveled it. They had guaranteed that.

"Good lord," a man said in the back in posh British English. "We're only three weeks from the trial date. What the hell are we supposed to do?"

"Shut the fuck up," an American man answered. "Can't you see we got injured here?"

And dying, Parker thought, but didn't say. Only this guy wasn't going to die any time soon. He would just die slowly, in more pain than Parker ever wanted to imagine.

"This isn't going to happen in the prison wing is it?" the Brit asked. "Because—"

"I said shut the fuck up," the American snapped.

"Perhaps you should take the argument elsewhere."

Parker recognized that voice. It belonged to Nathalie. She was also speaking English, this time with just a hint of a New England boarding school accent, one that conveyed both culture and command.

"We have a bit of a crisis here," she said, "and we don't need you two arguing over it. So either be useful or be gone."

Had the circumstances been just slightly different, Parker would have smiled. Instead, he crouched.

"We'll get you out of here," he said to the injured man in German.

Nathalie crouched beside him. He had no idea how she had made it through the debris. Maybe in his haste to clear it, he had created a path.

"My god," she said quietly.

Parker raised his head. She had gotten some of the dust off her face, so that she looked more like herself.

Her gaze met his, and he realized in that moment that she knew what was facing the man in front of them.

She shook her head slightly.

Parker shrugged. "Why don't you get the medics over here?" he said in French.

She nodded, then stood, picking her way back across the debris. He heard her tell someone to bring a stretcher.

He stayed beside the worker, talking quietly to him. It only took a few moments for medics to arrive.

Parker was glad they would work on the man. Parker didn't want to be near him as he died.

Parker stood, wiped his hands on his trousers, then saw Nathalie. She was farther away than he expected, deep in the pile of debris. He picked his way over to her, looking for more wounded, more bodies.

She was crouching near a man who looked amazingly unharmed. His left hand was pinned, but the rest of his body seemed fine—or would have, if his eyes weren't glazed and staring.

Still, Parker did what he had been doing all along, and touched the man's neck. His skin was still warm, but he wasn't breathing.

"Medic!" Parker shouted. "We need a medic!"

Nathalie touched Parker's arm. "He's dead. Leave him."

"He might have a blocked airway." Parker tilted the man's head back. He had learned this early in the war. He grabbed the jaw, forced it open, and Nathalie pushed at him.

"He's a Nazi," she said softly but with such force that Parker was reminded of the way she had spoken in that garden in Paris.

"You don't know that," Parker said. He glanced at the man. He was wearing the work clothes assigned to the civilians.

"I do know it," she said. "Leave him."

Parker shook his head. Nathalie pushed against him again.

"Back off," Parker said.

"You can do nothing," she said. "He is dead."

The man's eyes agreed with that, but Parker had seen men revived in the strangest of circumstances. He pried the man's mouth open, and saw a large splinter of wood inside. It made him shudder.

At that moment, two medics arrived.

"We got him," one of the medics said.

And Parker moved away. So did Nathalie.

"What the hell was that?" he snapped as soon as they were out of earshot.

A range of emotions crossed her face, almost as if she was practicing a variety of answers. Then she shrugged.

"You would call it—How do you say?—God's will," she said.

"God helps those who help themselves," Parker said, quoting his mother. He was rather surprised to hear those words come out of his own mouth.

"Yes," Nathalie said with a smile. "He does, doesn't He?"

And then she walked away, moving carefully through the debris.

Parker stared after her, feeling as unsettled as he had the first time he'd seen her.

She was beautiful, and she was talented, and, he realized, he didn't like her.

He didn't like her at all.

10

FORTUNATELY, HE DIDN'T HAVE TO MANAGE HER. THAT task fell to Felton because they decided to assign her to the Russians, whether they liked it or not.

"They deserve her," Felton said "They're being difficult."

So was she. She turned down three different rooms because she did not like the beds. When told she didn't have a choice, she confessed that she was allergic to certain types of metal. She would sleep anywhere so long as the bed frame was made of wood.

Parker got all the reports, but he ignored them. He had looked at her file, saw that his name was not on it as the person who recommended her to come to Nuremberg.

In fact, the file listed her as someone who walked in and volunteered. Her tests were so impressive that she was offered work on the spot, despite her sketchy paperwork.

Her work was impressive as well. She translated documents rapidly, helping the Russian section catch up, but she was the best in the Russian section at simultaneous translation. Unlike most simultaneous translators, her work was precise. The team that vetted the tapes of her comments said she always chose the right word.

None of the other simultaneous translators had such a perfect record.

But no one claimed her. No one said they were in the office when she arrived. People had given her tests, and had signed off, but no one claimed they had discovered her.

He didn't either. In fact, he never mentioned the encounter in Paris. He didn't want anyone to think he had something to do with her.

It soon became clear that everyone disliked her—and some of that dislike bordered on active hatred.

Not even Parker liked her, and he felt as if he should. He found her unbelievably attractive, and he enjoyed watching her from across the room. Her movements were graceful, her voice musical even when speaking harsh guttural languages, and her smile was so stunning that it took his breath away.

But he didn't want to get near her. He tried to pretend she wasn't there.

Not that it was hard. He was busier than ever. The collapse of the floor in the courtroom provided an opportunity for the translation division to supervise the installation of the simultaneous translation equipment.

Parker was often at the courtroom, pouring over the architectural drawings, trying to figure out where the cables would go. He wanted the cables laid in the floor, but Dostert had nixed that. Dostert believed the system might need to be moved, and he didn't want to be tied to any position.

Parker was worried that someone would trip as they walked past the translation tables. Everyone would be wearing headphones, and those headphones would have cords as well. It was, he thought, a nightmare of cables and wires and connections, and he wanted to minimize them as much as he could.

He was working with one of the construction supervisors when he caught the man staring at the floor. It had been rebuilt, and looked sturdy. The entire courtroom looked sturdy, and for the first time, he had the sense that it would be ready to go when needed.

"It looks good," he said. "I don't think we have to worry about it collapsing this time."

Everyone looked at him. No one spoke of the collapse. Three workers had died, and several had been injured. Some of the injured hadn't yet returned.

"It looked good before," the supervisor said. "We had shored it up properly. I don't know what went wrong."

Two of the German workers also stood near the door. One of them said softly to the other, in German, "What went wrong is simple. They should never have let her up here."

"Who?" Parker asked.

"That woman," he said. "The faerie."

Parker frowned. The German word was clear, and had none of the double meanings found in English. *Fee*. Faerie. Magical creature.

"Excuse me," he said. "I don't understand. What woman?"

"You do not see her?" the German asked. "I have seen you talking to her."

"She is with the Russians now," the second German said.

"Why did you call her a faerie?"

The German gave him a withering look. "Because that is what she is."

Parker glanced at the others. The construction supervisor had moved into the courtroom, and was studying the dark paneling. Some of the other workers had moved to the judge's bench, which was being built in front of the large windows. Parker hadn't liked that either—he didn't think it safe to have the judges in front of windows—but he hadn't even gotten a vote.

The justices wanted everything to look impressive in photographs, and having the velvet curtains behind the bench was a great deal more impressive than the carvings on the paneling.

He frowned. No one else had heard the comment. And he didn't know how to interpret it. Germans had a lot of insults for a variety of people, and while he was good at the language, he didn't know all of the regional idioms. For all he knew, *Fee* was some kind of insult that had more than one meaning.

But he also knew the Germans were superstitious. They were the ones who had codified what were, in English, fairy tales, and many of those tales were set in actual German towns and villages. Many Germans—even before the war—swore the tales were real, and Parker had never known whether or not to take those Germans seriously. They did, after all, like to bait Americans.

Still, the worker hadn't initially made the comment to Parker. He had made the comment to his friend.

Parker sighed and shook it off. If he responded to every bit of German bigotry, every comment about the glory days of the Reich that he heard from the employees at the Grand Hotel, he would spend his days screaming at Germans.

They were conquered, just like General Eisenhower had said, but they weren't entirely defeated. And even those that were seemed to think they hadn't done anything wrong.

11

A WEEK BEFORE THE TRIAL BEGAN, HE SAW HER IN THE Grand Hotel. She wore a beautiful red velvet dress that made her seem so bright, she looked like a beacon from across the lobby. She wore long white gloves, and it wasn't until Parker got close to her that he realized both the gloves had been darned and the velvet on the dress had mostly rubbed off.

Still, she was the most gorgeous woman in the lobby, and apparently, someone did like her, because she was on the arm of a Russian officer that Parker didn't recognize. They were heading to the Marble Room, where the entertainment that night was supposed to be American jazz.

Parker wondered how the Russian got permission to go to an American event. Many of the Russian delegation had been sent away because they fraternized too much with the West. Many of the good Russian translators who had arrived late had already been sent away.

Parker tried not to talk to the good translators remaining, unwilling to contaminate them in the eyes of their superiors.

The Marble Room was the premiere night club—if one could call anything that—in Nuremberg, but only high-ranking officers and VIPs were allowed inside. Parker had gotten permission more than a month before to go into the Marble Room, but once inside, he realized it was not an experience he wanted to repeat.

The music was good, but he could hear that through the walls. Hardly anyone danced because there weren't enough women, and so mostly the men sat at little round tables, watched the entertainment and drank. Usually there were some German women near the bandstand. Parker recognized them from his walks. Some of the officers thought them prostitutes and treated them as such. Parker knew they took the money.

He also knew they would starve if they did not.

They, more than anything, kept him out of the room. He knew what was happening, but he didn't have to watch.

This time, however, he went in. The Russian was trying to find a table. Nathalie waited by the door.

"I see you've made yourself at home," he said in French.

She turned. "The Russians are the only ones who will talk to me."

"Maybe you should stop giving your opinions about the Tribunal," Parker said.

She smiled slightly. "I have not said a word to anyone since Paris."

Not since she spoke to him, in other words.

"Yet you're here. Does that mean you've changed your mind?"

The Russian was talking with one of the British officers near the dance floor. Parker kept an eye on him, ready to move if he had to.

"Changed my mind?" Nathalie asked. "About the fate of the defendants? Of course not. In fact, once I learned who they were, I decided I could not stay away."

"Even though this won't be a show trial? I suspect that some of them will not be found guilty."

"As a matter of course," she said, watching the Russian as well, "even if they are all guilty, you will set some free to prove a silly point."

"*I* won't," he said.

"You pretend you are not involved," she said. "But you are in the middle of this thing."

"So are you," he said.

She looked at him sideways. The music was starting up. The band members had arrived.

"We all have our own ways to get revenge." Her voice was soft, and he wasn't sure he heard her correctly. He was about to ask her what she meant when the Russian returned.

"I beg your pardon," he said to Parker in heavily accented English, then extended his arm to Nathalie.

She slipped her hand in the crook of his arm, and smiled at Parker. As they walked away, the band launched into swing.

Swing. Such upbeat music.

Yet inside that room, no one even pretended to have a good time.

12

THE FINAL WEEK BEFORE THE TRIAL BEGAN GOT CRAZY. Parker spent much of his day with the simultaneous translators, working with them on the in-court system, making sure they could handle the switches, making sure they could talk and listen while others spoke different languages around them.

The security at the Palace of Justice was so tight that he finally gave up walking and rode with some of the others from the Grand Hotel. That way, he could get inside quickly, without a prolonged stop in front of the MPs.

More than 300 members of the worldwide press had shown up, and there were only 240 seats for journalists in the courtroom. Someone got the bright idea to set up a press palace at Stein Castle, along with rooms and a place to go for information. The military provided Jeeps to take the pool reporters back and forth.

The press department worried about the press releases. The translation division simply had to make sure the releases were in the proper languages.

But Parker had to go to Stein Castle twice that week to set up translators for the most important guests. It irritated him; he still felt as if they were short on translators and the last people he wanted to waste them on was the press.

Still, he did his job. Without the press, the world would not know about the trial, but he couldn't help thinking of Nathalie and her remarks about show trials. He was beginning to resent the demands on his time, the seeming impossibility of this task with no guaranteed outcome.

He found himself wondering if execution wasn't simpler, easier, and saner.

But he said nothing to anyone about it. And late one night, shortly before the trial, he found himself in the makeshift bar in Stein Castle, with some people who would have once impressed him—John Steinbeck, Ernest Hemingway, and John Dos Passos. Instead, Parker couldn't stand to listen to their conversation, which saw only the superficial parts of Nuremberg and not the city underneath.

He moved away, listened to William Shirer discuss Germany before the war and Germany now, and decided he couldn't take much more of that conversation either. Still, Parker had a beer to finish, and this was the first time he had been off his feet all day.

He closed his eyes for half a moment, when a chair squeaked beside him. He opened his eyes and instantly regretted it.

The man across from him was named Joe Decker. He was an American who had gone to Paris to write a novel in the 1920s and had never ever gone home. Instead of writing his novel, Decker had gotten a job with a Paris paper Parker had heard about but never seen, *Noir: The Newspaper of the City of Dark*.

People often talked about *Noir*, about its skewed perspective, and he had asked for a copy more than once. But no one had ever provided one. A number of people had told him he clearly hadn't qualified for the paper yet.

He didn't know how a man qualified for a newspaper if he only wanted to read it. He'd always meant to ask Decker that, but never had the chance.

Decker himself was strange. He was so gaunt he looked ill, and his eyes were shrunken into his head. In the middle of a conversation, those eyes would often go blank, as if he was seeing something no one else could see. Sometimes he would shake himself and continue speaking as if nothing happened, and sometimes he would use the edge of the table to help himself up, mumble something about needing to write, and flee.

Decker didn't drink, although every time Parker had seen him, they'd been in a bar. Decker would often stare at the booze around him like a starving man stared at a buffet.

"So tell me," Decker said without saying hello, "how you came to hire Nathalie Renard."

Parker started. No one knew that he had even interviewed Nathalie. "I didn't hire her."

"You interviewed her in Paris, and now she's here. How in God's name did you get a woman like that to work for you?"

"I didn't," Parker said. "She came on her own."

"After you hired her."

Parker shook his head. "I thought about it, but we never got past the initial interview. Then she turned up here."

Decker grunted. He grabbed some peanuts off a nearby table, and ate them, shell and all.

"Why do you care?" Parker asked.

Decker's eyes glinted. "You don't know what she is, do you?"

"I know her family was killed in the camps. She belongs to one of those groups the Nazis considered undesirable. If I had to guess, I'd say she was a gypsy, but I have no idea." Then he thought of the workers, thought he might ask Decker about that strange use of the word "fee," and then decided against it.

"You believe in magic, Parker?" Decker asked.

Parker laughed. Of course he believed in magic—the kind any beautiful woman had. Nathalie Renard had more of it than most lovely women—until you talked to her.

Decker wasn't laughing. He had leaned forward.

"I mean it, Parker. Do you believe in magic?"

"No," Parker said. "Why would I?"

"Because you have a faerie working for you."

Same word, different language. Parker smiled. "You're strange, Decker. You really are."

"I'm serious," he said. "Didn't you read Grimm? Faeries are dangerous creatures."

"You're talking about Nathalie, right? Am I missing something? Some kind of slang?" Although he couldn't imagine what it would be, not in English and in German.

"She wasn't lying to you about her family," Decker said. "The Nazis targeted anything magical. If they couldn't use the magic to their advantage, they destroyed it."

Parker sighed. "There's no such thing as magic. If there had been magic, there would have been no Hitler."

Decker raised his eyebrows, giving him an almost comical look of surprise. "Where did you get that idea?"

"Oh, hell, I don't know," Parker said. "The Nazis couldn't have destroyed magic. If it had been real, no one could have tampered with it."

Decker ran a hand over his face, glanced over his shoulder, and said, "It's not that simple. Mostly the magic folk avoid the human realm. They did what they did, and we did what we did, and sometimes there was connection, but mostly there wasn't. They live longer than we do, and they have fewer children, and their magic fades with time."

Parker grabbed his beer. Decker really was serious. And crazy. Seriously crazy.

"By the time they figured out what was going on, it was too late," Decker said.

"So that's when they waved their magic wands and stopped Hitler," Parker said, wishing he could figure out a way to end this conversation.

"It wasn't that simple. It wasn't a coincidence that the Nazis used iron in almost everything."

"What?" Parker asked.

"Iron," Decker said. "It's the only thing that binds faeries. It interferes with their magic."

Parker shook his head. "Give it a rest, Decker. You do know where Nathalie was working when I met her, right?"

"The Paris Telephone Exchange."

"And you do know that the equipment there is made of metal."

Decker nodded. "And our girl wore gloves even in the summer, and tried not to touch any metal directly even then."

Parker froze. He remembered those gloves. Then he shook that detail off. The key to any good story was the right detail. Of course, Decker knew that.

"If she had magic, she could have rescued her family. They would have been all right."

"She's the descendant of wood nymphs," Decker said. "If she did any magic at all, she would have to use wood as a conduit. She can't do anything directly. Think about it: How do you defeat a machine with wood?"

He had an answer for everything. No beer was worth this conversation. Parker set the stein down.

"Fun as this was, Decker," he said, "I'm exhausted, and I have a hundred things to do before the trial starts. For the record, whatever she is, Nathalie Renard is the best linguist I have ever encountered, and we're happy to have her."

"She doesn't learn languages," Decker said. "She taps into them. That's the other side of her magic, this facility with words. Faeries have charm, Parker—"

"She's not charming," he said as he stood. "She's annoying. But I have to say, she's not nearly as annoying as you are."

And then he walked away.

He wasn't supposed to be rude to the press, but he couldn't help himself. Besides, how could anyone think Decker was press? *Noir: The Newspaper For The City of Dark.* Who took that seriously? Who took any of it seriously?

He'd have a talk with whoever gave Decker a press pass.

When he had the chance. Which wasn't this night.

This night, he staggered out to the parking area and found one of the Jeeps, complete with driver.

"Take me to the Grand Hotel," he said, and hoped, after that conversation, he'd still be able to get at least a few hours of dreamless sleep.

13

OF COURSE, HE WASN'T THAT LUCKY. HE DID DREAM, mostly of Nathalie's face in that first interview, the way her eyes went flat, the almost literal sharpness to her words. In his dreams, she wore gloves, and she had put them back on in the basement of the Palace of Justice as she held splinters of wood.

He woke up in a cold sweat. As much as he tried to ignore the emotions around him, the fear, the turmoil, the anger, and the loss, he couldn't. It was too much, even for him.

He got up, showered, and dressed in his uniform, just like he had been instructed to do. Then he went downstairs and ordered a car, figuring someone else would be up at four in the morning.

On this morning, anyway.

With the trial about to begin.

14

THE PX INSIDE THE PALACE OF JUSTICE WAS OPEN, AND just like he suspected, he wasn't the only one unable to sleep. Many of the guards were already here, as well as some of the lawyers. A few people had seen Dostert, who said he was going to the courtroom to check and recheck the translation system.

After eating a breakfast of unbelievably greasy eggs, Parker washed it down with thin coffee. Before checking in at the translation division, he decided to go up to the courtroom to see if Dostert needed help.

In a few hours, everyone would be here: the world press, the justices, the prosecutors, and of course, the defendants themselves. Parker had already heard of Göring attempting to bend the Tribunal to his own rather twisted wishes.

Guards were everywhere, on every floor, in every stairwell. Years ago, Parker would have thought that excessive. But now he knew it would take a single bomb to make a statement for the Reich, or just a few gunshots, something to disrupt this revival of civilization, as Armed Forces Radio was calling it.

No one wanted that.

As he climbed that last flight of stairs, he thought he saw a flash of skirt. Nathalie? Possibly. Maybe Dostert had been using her to help him test the equipment.

But Parker didn't remember ever seeing Dostert interacting with Nathalie, and he didn't think Felton would recommend her for the job.

Parker's heart pounded. She had no real reason to be up here, did she?

These men have ruined the world, she had said.

They deserve death.

He climbed faster, taking the stairs two at a time. He passed a guard, and then another.

"Did you see a woman go by?" he asked.

The guard nodded. "She had a pass," he said.

His breath caught.

They should never have let her up here, one of the German workers said. *That woman. The faerie.*

He rounded the corner.

I mean it, Parker. Do you believe in magic?

He didn't. He never had.

So why was his heart pounding so hard?

He hurried down the corridor, past the locked double doors and the guards outside. There was a back entrance, one that Dostert preferred. It was just around the corner, half hidden by the wall.

And as Parker approached, he saw two gloves, resting one on top of the other.

He held his breath, walked as quietly as he could, wondering if the guards could hear his heart pounding. From inside the courtroom, he heard Dostert's voice, saying that they needed to try again, it had to be right the first time.

Parker rounded the corner, and stopped. She was on her knees, her hand touching the joint where the floor met the wall. The wall was plaster and lathe.

The floor, beneath the carpet, was wood.

If she did any magic at all, Decker had said, *she would have to use wood as a conduit.*

And she had been up here weeks ago, just minutes before the floor collapsed. The floor that had looked fine.

The floor that had tumbled through three stories, into the basement, killing three men—killing one by lodging a wooden splinter in his throat.

Parker took one more step to the side. Her hand was lost inside the floor. It looked like the floor had eaten her skin.

Until he squinted, saw her hand inside like a photographic negative. He could actually see the bits of wood separating from other bits of wood, as if she were somehow loosening the bonds that held the wood itself together.

That would make wood shred. Any additional weight on the floor—defendants, judges, *people*—and the wood would give way.

How many would die when they fell three stories?

And how many would she be down there to kill? To get her revenge.

He didn't think about it. He dove for her, grabbed her, and pulled her away.

He felt something—a power, an energy, almost as if he had put his finger in an electrical socket, and then he tumbled with her, away from the wood, all the way to the marble floor.

"Let me go," she said in German. "Let me go. You don't know what they did. They killed everyone. Everyone I knew. You cannot be fair. You cannot let them go. You cannot let them *live*."

He kept shoving her, moving her as far away from the wood as he could, wishing he had thought to bring something metal.

"Let me go," she said again. "You understand. I know you do."

That froze him for just a moment.

She scrambled out from underneath him, crawled toward the door, and he grabbed her ankle.

"No," he said. "You'll kill everyone in that room."

"Because you're going to let them go free," she said.

He had no answer for that. She shook her leg, reached for his hands, trying to free herself.

"Hey!" he shouted in English. "I need help here."

But someone was already running toward them. The guards he had seen, running, and staring at her, trying to claw her way to that room.

"She's trying to set up a trap for the defendants," Parker said, hoping he wouldn't have to explain any more. "Do you have handcuffs?"

Military police. Of course they had handcuffs. One of them reached down, grabbed her hand, and yelped in pain. She was giving off that energy again, almost like sparks of light.

Parker didn't care. He took the handcuffs from the guard, and snapped them on her wrists.

She wilted and, for the first time, looked haggard. "You don't know what you're doing," she said. "They'll go free."

"That's the risk," he said. "That was always the risk."

15

THEY TOOK HER OUT, AWAY FROM THE PALACE OF JUSTICE. Parker insisted she leave Nuremberg: he was afraid she would get too close to the prisoners, again.

But he didn't say that. He just told the guards it was better to have her as far away from the proceedings as possible.

No one inside the courtroom had heard the struggle. Dostert's test continued. Parker couldn't go inside.

Instead, he picked up her gloves. Darned and frayed, they looked tattered and old. Like she had as the guard dragged her away.

You understand, she had said. And he did. God help him, he did.

And he didn't want to think about it. So he promised himself he wouldn't.

He went back down the stairs slowly, like an old man. Halfway down, he realized he had to let someone know about the floor, so he told one of the guards he had seen the woman that was just arrested tampering with an area near the door.

"It needs to be examined," he said, and he hoped that would be enough.

He trusted it would.

He went into the translation division, startled to see so many people already at work. Felton was there. He didn't ask why Parker had arrived so early. Instead, he thrust a document at him.

"Jackson gave us his opening statement," Felton said. "He's reading it tomorrow. We need to translate it and it's a goddamn novel."

"You want me to translate?" Parker asked. His brain was moving slowly.

"English to German. Just a section, until some more people in the documents division get here. Okay?"

Parker nodded. He took the section to one of the desks, grabbed some paper, and sat down. The desk was littered with magazines and newspapers. As he moved them, one of the newspapers tumbled to the floor.

He bent over to pick it up, and then his hand stopped.

Last night's edition of *Noir* with the headline: *Justice in a Haunted City*.

It looked like a real newspaper. Felt like one too.

He picked up the paper and set it aside. He couldn't read French right now. Right now, he needed to concentrate on English.

He needed to concentrate on something.

He read the line at the top of the page:

We must never forget, Justice Jackson had written, *that the record on which we judge these defendants today is the record on which history will judge us tomorrow.*

"Amen," Parker said softly, wishing he could show that to Nathalie. "Amen."

About the Author

USA Today bestselling author Kristine Kathryn Rusch writes in almost every genre. Generally, she uses her real name (Rusch) for most of her writing. Under that name, she publishes bestselling science fiction and fantasy, award-winning mysteries, acclaimed mainstream fiction, controversial nonfiction, and the occasional romance. Her novels have made bestseller lists around the world and her short fiction has appeared in eighteen best of the year collections. She has won more than twenty-five awards for her fiction, including the Hugo, *Le Prix Imaginales,* the *Asimov's* Readers Choice award, and the *Ellery Queen Mystery Magazine* Readers Choice Award.

To keep up with everything she does, go to kristine kathrynrusch.com and sign up for her newsletter. To track her many pen names and series, see their individual websites (krisnelscott.com, kristinegrayson.com, krisdelake. com, retrievalartist.com, divingintothewreck.com). She lives and occasionally sleeps in Oregon.

Be the first to know!

Just sign up for the Kristine Kathryn Rusch newsletter, and keep up with the latest news, releases and so much more—even the occasional giveaway.

To sign up, go to kristinekathrynrusch.com.

But wait! There's more. Sign up for the WMG Publishing newsletter, too, and get the latest news and releases from all of the WMG authors and lines, including Kristine Grayson, Kris Nelscott, Dean Wesley Smith, *Fiction River: An Original Anthology Magazine, Smith's Monthly,* and so much more.

Just go to wmgpublishing.com and click on Newsletter.

Read more Faerie Justice stories
in *The War and After: Five Stories of Magic & Revenge,*
available from your favorite bookseller.